STECK-VAUGHN

PAIR-IT BOOKS™

Beach Creatures

Written by Michael K. Smith

STECK-VAUGHN
C O M P A N Y
A Division of Harcourt Brace & Company

There are many interesting beach creatures.
Can you name them?
Read the clues to see if you can guess.

I am a round circle. I look like a coin.

You cannot spend me.

What am I?

I am a sand dollar.

I live in sandy places, but I'm not a dollar.

I have five points. I do not shine.

I do not live in the sky.

What am I?

I am a starfish.
I look like a star, but I'm not a fish.

I spear and saw my food. I cannot saw wood.
You cannot use me to build anything.
What am I?

I am a sawfish.
I am a fish, but I'm not a saw.

I have a hidden treasure inside.

I can open and close.

What am I?

I am an oyster.

I can make a pearl, but I cannot make

a whole necklace.

I have a head that looks like a horse.
I swim standing up.
What am I?

I am a sea horse.

I live in the sea, but I'm not a horse.

I look like jelly. I have no bones.
I can open and close like an umbrella.
What am I?

I am a jellyfish.
I look like jelly, but I'm not a fish.

I play in the ocean. I ride the waves.
I am not a fish.
What am I?

I am a surfer!